To Marley Kathleen Burroughs
S. M.

To Alexander and Maria Brodsky with love
B. I.

Text copyright © 2007 by Stephen Mitchell
Illustrations copyright © 2007 by Bagram Ibatoulline

First edition 2007

Library of Congress Cataloging-in-Publication Data is available.

Library of Congress Catalog Card Number 2006047554

ISBN 978-0-7636-2078-3

2 4 6 8 10 9 7 5 3 1

Printed in China

This book was typeset in Barbedor.
The illustrations were done in watercolor and pen and ink.

Candlewick Press
2067 Massachusetts Avenue
Cambridge, Massachusetts 02140

visit us at www.candlewick.com

HANS CHRISTIAN ANDERSEN

THE TINDERBOX

retold by

STEPHEN MITCHELL

illustrated by

BAGRAM IBATOULLINE

CANDLEWICK PRESS
CAMBRIDGE, MASSACHUSETTS

A soldier came marching along the road: *Left, right! Left, right!* He had his knapsack on his back and a sword at his side because he had been to the war and now he was on his way home.

As he marched along, he met an old witch on the road. She was very ugly, and her lower lip hung down to her breast.

"Good evening, soldier," she said. "What a fine sword you have, and what a big knapsack! You look just the way a soldier should. Now I'll show you how to get as much money as you want."

"Thank you, old witch," said the soldier.

"Do you see that big tree over there?" the witch said, pointing. "It's completely hollow inside. If you climb to the top, you'll see a hole, and you can crawl through the hole and lower yourself down to the bottom. I'll tie a rope around your waist, and I'll pull you up again when you tell me to."

"But what am I supposed to do once I'm down there in the tree?" the soldier said.

"Get money," said the witch. "When you reach the bottom, you'll find yourself in a large hall. It will be very bright, with hundreds of lamps burning. Then you'll see three doors. The keys are in the locks, so you'll be able to open them. When you enter the first room, you'll see a large chest in the middle of the floor, and on it will be a dog with eyes as big as clocks. But don't worry about him. I'll give you my blue-checked apron. Spread it on the floor, then grab the dog, put him on my apron, open the chest, and take as much money as you want. The coins are just copper.

"If you'd rather have silver coins, you'll have to go into the second room, where you'll find a dog with eyes as big as dinner plates. But don't worry about him. Put him on my apron, and then take as much money as you want.

"But if you'd rather have gold, you can have that too, as much as you can carry. Just go into the third room, where there's another chest full of gold. But the dog on this chest has eyes as big as wagon wheels. He is quite a dog, believe me! But don't be scared. Put him on my apron, and he won't hurt you. Take as much gold as you want."

"That's not a bad deal," said the soldier. "But what am I supposed to give you? You're not telling me all this for nothing."

"No," the witch said, "but I won't ask you for a single penny. Just bring me an old tinderbox that my grandmother forgot the last time she went down there."

"All right," the soldier said. "Now tie the rope around my waist."

"Here it is," said the witch. "And here's my blue-checked apron."

The soldier climbed up the tree, went through the hole, lowered himself down to the bottom, and found himself, just as the witch had said, in a large hall where hundreds of lamps were burning.

Then he opened the first door. Oh! There sat the dog with eyes as big as clocks, staring at him.

"*You're* a fine fellow!" said the soldier. He grabbed the dog, put him on the witch's apron, took as many copper coins as he could stuff into his pockets, closed the chest, put the dog back on it, and walked into the next room.

Ooh! There sat the dog with eyes as big as dinner plates.

"You'd better not stare at me that way," said the soldier, "or you'll strain your eyes." And he put the dog on the witch's apron. But when he saw the piles of silver coins in the chest, he threw away all the copper coins he'd taken, and he filled his pockets and his knapsack with silver.

Then he walked into the third room. What a hideous sight! The dog here really did have eyes as big as wagon wheels, and they turned around and around in his head.

"Good evening," said the soldier, and he touched his cap because never in his life had he seen a dog like this. But after he let the dog stare at him for a while, he said to himself, *Enough of that!* and he put him on the apron and opened the chest. Ooh! Dear God, what a lot of gold there was inside! Enough to buy the whole city of Copenhagen and all the candy in it, and all the tin soldiers and hoops and rocking horses in the whole world. So the soldier threw away all the silver coins he'd taken, and he replaced them with gold. He filled his pockets and his knapsack and his cap and his boots so full that he could hardly walk. Now he was really rich! He put the dog back on the chest, closed the door, and shouted up through the tree, "Pull me out now, old witch!"

"Do you have the tinderbox?" asked the witch.

"Oh, I completely forgot it," the soldier said. So he went back and found it.

The witch pulled him up out of the tree, and there he was again, standing on the road, with his pockets, knapsack, cap, and boots filled with gold.

"What are you going to do with the tinderbox?" asked the soldier.

"That's none of your business!" the witch said. "You've got your money. Give me the tinderbox, or else . . ."

"Fiddledeedee!" the soldier said. "Don't threaten me, or I'll draw my sword and cut off your head."

"I dare you!" said the witch.

So he cut her head off. Her body fell to the ground, and her head fell beside it. Then he tied up all his money in her apron, slung it over his shoulder, put the tinderbox in his pocket, and walked straight to town.

It was a splendid town, and he went to the best inn and stayed in the best room and ordered his favorite dishes, because he was so rich now that he could afford anything he wanted. The servant who had to clean his boots said to himself that for such a rich gentleman, this was an awfully shabby pair of boots (the soldier hadn't had time to buy new ones). The next day, though, he bought himself new boots and some elegant new clothes. Now the soldier had become a fine gentleman, and the people told him about all the sights of their town, and about their king, and what a lovely princess his daughter was.

"Where can I see her?" asked the soldier.

"She can't be seen at all," they said. "She lives in a big copper castle, surrounded by walls and towers. No one but the king is allowed to see her because a fortuneteller once predicted that she'd marry a common soldier, and kings don't like to hear things like that."

I really want to see her, the soldier thought, but there was no way to do it.

His life was very pleasant now. He was always going to the theater or riding in the park, and he gave lots of money to the poor, which was very kind of him (he remembered how hard it had been in the old days, when he was poor himself). He had beautiful clothes and many friends, who all said that he was an excellent fellow—a true gentleman—and the soldier loved to hear that.

But since he spent a lot of money every day and didn't make any to replace it, the moment soon came when he had just two coins left. So he had to leave his beautiful rooms and live in a cramped little attic under the roof. He had to clean his own boots and mend them with a darning needle, and none of his friends ever came to see him (there were too many stairs to climb).

One dark evening, when he couldn't afford to buy even a candle, he suddenly remembered that there was a little piece of a candle in the tinderbox that the witch had asked him to bring from the old tree. He got out the tinderbox and the piece of candle, but the moment he struck a spark from the flint and steel, the door flew open and the dog with eyes as big as clocks stood before him and said, "Master, what is your command?"

My, my, thought the soldier, *this is quite a tinderbox if it gets me whatever I want.* "Bring me some money," he said to the dog, and *whooshhh!* the dog was gone, and *whooshhh!* he was back again, carrying a large bag of copper coins in his mouth.

Now the soldier realized what a marvelous tinderbox it was. When he struck the flint twice, he brought the dog who sat on the chest of silver coins; three times, the dog who sat on the chest of gold coins; four times, all the dogs together.

The soldier lost no time in moving back to his beautiful rooms and changing back into his fine clothes, and all his friends recognized him right away and were as fond of him as before.

One day he said to himself, *It's awfully strange that no one's allowed to see the princess. People say she's very beautiful, but what good is that if she always has to sit in the copper castle surrounded by all those towers? There must be some way I can get to see her. Wait a minute! Where's my tinderbox?* Then he struck a light, and *whooshhh!* there stood the dog with eyes as big as clocks.

"I know it's the middle of the night," said the soldier, "but I would really like to see the princess, if only for a moment."

In a flash the dog was out the door, and before the soldier had time to think, the dog returned with the princess. She was lying asleep on the dog's back, and she was so lovely that anyone could see she was a real princess. The soldier couldn't help it—he leaned over and gave her a kiss (that's what soldiers are like).

Then the dog ran back with the princess. But in the morning, at breakfast with the king and queen, the princess said that she'd had a very strange dream, about a dog and a soldier. She had ridden on the dog's back, and the soldier had kissed her.

"What a peculiar story!" said the queen.

SO THE NEXT NIGHT the king and queen had one of the old ladies-in-waiting sit up all night by the princess's bed, to find out if it was really a dream or not.

The soldier longed to see the beautiful princess again, so at night the dog came, took her, and ran as fast as he could. But the old lady-in-waiting put on her overboots and ran just as fast after them. When she saw them disappear into a big house, she thought, *Now I know where it is*, and with a piece of chalk she drew a large cross on the door. Then she went home to bed, and the dog came back with the princess. But when the dog saw that someone had made a cross on the door where the soldier lived, he took another piece of chalk and made crosses on every door in the town. That was very clever of him, because now the old lady-in-waiting wouldn't be able to find the right door, since there were crosses on all of them.

Early the next morning, the king and queen, the old lady-in-waiting, and all the court officials went out to see where the princess had been.

"Here it is," the king said when they came to the first door with a cross on it.

"No, my dear, this must be the one," said the queen, pointing to a second door with a cross.

"But here's another, and there's another!" they all kept saying, because whichever way they turned, there were crosses on the doors. So they realized that it would be pointless to look any farther.

But the queen was an extremely clever woman; she could do more than just ride in a carriage. She took her big gold scissors, cut a piece of silk into squares, and sewed them into a pretty little bag, which she filled with the finest buckwheat flour. She fastened the bag to the princess's back and then punched a small hole in the bag so that the flour would be scattered along whatever path the princess took.

That night the dog came again, took the princess on his back, and ran off with her to the soldier, who loved her very much and wished he were a prince so that he could marry her.

The dog never noticed how the flour leaked out from the castle wall all the way to the window of the soldier's house. So in the morning, the king and queen could easily see where their daughter had been, and they had the soldier arrested and put in prison.

There he sat. It was dark and dreary, and the jailer kept saying to him, "Tomorrow they're going to hang you." That wasn't very pleasant news, and besides, he had left the tinderbox at the inn.

In the morning, through the iron bars of his little window, he watched people hurrying out of the town to see him hanged. He heard the drums and saw the soldiers marching past. Everyone was going out to see the hanging. Among the crowd there was a shoemaker's boy in a leather apron and slippers, who galloped by so fast that one of his slippers flew off and hit the wall where the soldier sat looking through the iron bars.

"Hey, there! No need to be in such a hurry," the soldier said. "They can't start without me. Listen now: If you'll run over to my inn and bring me my tinderbox, I'll give you four pennies. But you'll have to be very quick about it." The shoemaker's boy was glad to earn four pennies, so he ran and got the tinderbox and gave it to the soldier. And now you'll hear what happened.

Outside the town, a high gallows had been built, and all around it stood the soldiers, and thousands and thousands of people. The king and the queen sat on splendid thrones opposite the judges and all the councilors.

The soldier already stood on the ladder, but as they were about to put the rope around his neck, he reminded them that a criminal is always entitled to one last request and that *his* request was to smoke a pipe, one last time.

The king couldn't refuse him, so the soldier took out a pipe and took out his tinderbox and struck the flint, once, twice, three, four times—and there stood all three dogs, the one with eyes like clocks, the one with eyes like dinner plates, and the one with eyes like wagon wheels.

"Save me from being hanged!" said the soldier. And the dogs leaped onto the judges and councilors. They grabbed some by their legs, and others by their noses, and tossed them into the air so high that when they came down, their bones broke into many pieces and they all died.

"I will not be tossed!" said the king, but the biggest dog grabbed him, as well as the queen, and tossed them into the air like the others. Then the soldiers got frightened, and the people cried out, "Dear soldier, you shall be our king and marry the beautiful princess."

So they put the soldier in the king's carriage, and the three dogs jumped up and down and cried "Hooray!" and the little boys whistled through their fingers, and the soldiers presented arms. The princess came out of the copper castle and was made queen, which pleased her a lot. The wedding feast lasted for a whole week, and the dogs sat with them at the table and stared with all their eyes.